Postman Pat and a Job Well Done

SIMON AND SCHUSTER

Pat and Sara were having breakfast.

"Come on, Julian!" said Pat. "You'll be late for school!"

"No school this morning," said Sara. "Mr Pringle has given them a half-day. Ted Glen is varnishing the classroom floor!"

"Look what Jess has done to my computer mouse!" said Julian. "And I've got my class talk this afternoon."

Jess shot under the table to hide.

"I'm supposed to stand up in front of the whole class and talk about people's jobs," Julian moaned, "and now I won't be able to find anything out!"

"I could tell you about being a postman?" suggested Pat.

Julian sighed. "I need to know about *lots* of jobs."

"Well, come with me on my rounds this morning! I deliver to lots of different people. You can learn all about their jobs."

"OK! Thanks, Dad!" Julian said cheerfully.

Pat, Julian and Jess set off.

Mr Pringle and Ted were stacking up the desks and chairs in the school playground.

"Don't forget your class talk at twelve o'clock, Julian!" called Mr Pringle.

Pat loaded up his van at the Post Office. Mrs Goggins wished Julian good luck with his talk.

"The first delivery is for Reverend Timms," Pat told Julian. "You can ask him about his job."

"Great! I've got my notebook ready!" said Julian.

Reverend Timms was planting flower bulbs. Pat handed him a letter. "Doing a spot of gardening I see, Reverend?"

The vicar smiled. "Oh yes. All part of my duties."

"Really?" Julian asked, scribbling in his notebook. "What else do you have to do for your job?"

"Ah well now, I have to test the church bells to make sure they're tip-top for Sunday. You see this rope? It leads to the bells, and if you give it a tug, it makes them ring. Would you like to try, Julian?"

"Yes please!"

Julian grabbed the rope, gave it a pull – and flew up into the air. "Whoooa!"

Julian bounced up and down, as the bells rang loudly in the tower above, and Jess jumped onto Julian's leg to try and keep him on the ground.

"This is better than the funfair!" Julian laughed. "Thanks, Reverend Timms!"

Ted hadn't got very far with his varnishing.

Mr Pringle was worried. "The children are coming at twelve, Ted. Can you go a bit quicker? You'll never finish at this rate."

Ted scratched his head. "Aye, you could be right. Well, let's see now... yes! That'll do it. Have you got an old broom, Jeff?"

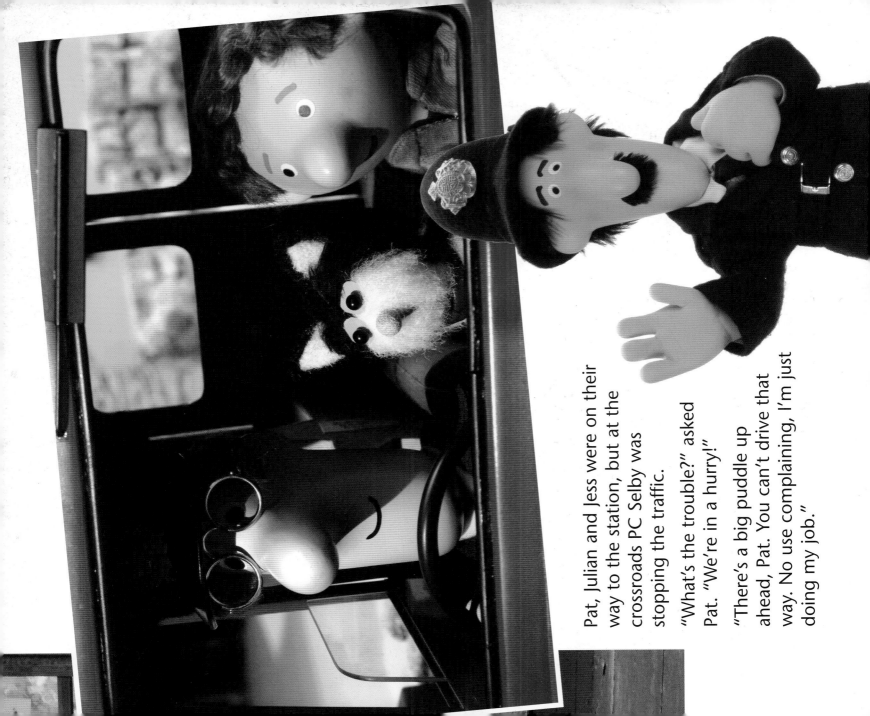

Pat, Julian and Jess were on their way to the station, but at the crossroads PC Selby was stopping the traffic.

"What's the trouble?" asked Pat. "We're in a hurry!"

"There's a big puddle up ahead, Pat. You can't drive that way. No use complaining, I'm just doing my job."

Julian jumped out of the van. "Brilliant! Tell me more about your job please, PC Selby."

"Well, I er . . . have to look for lost cats . . . and I er . . . have to direct the traffic, like this."

Julian picked up one of the road signs. "What's this arrow thing for?" he asked.

"Hey! Careful with that!" PC Selby frowned. "That arrow points the traffic in the right direction."

"Now which direction was it? This way? Or that way? Hmm, let me think now. It can't be that way. . . so is it this way. . .?"

Julian jumped back in the van, and Pat drove off, leaving PC Selby to decide which way the arrow should be pointing.

Back at school, Ted had completed his new invention: three brushes tied to a broom handle!

Jeff was impressed. "Now you can varnish three times as fast!"

"Aye, I'll have this floor finished in no time," Ted promised.

Ted brushed the varnish onto the floor. "Champion! This is grand!"

He didn't stop until he had varnished himself into a corner!

"Oh 'eck! I've gone and got myself stuck. I can't walk on this floor until it's dry."

Ted opened the cupboard door and stepped inside.

Then he sat down, yawned, and nodded off as the cupboard door swung shut. . . .

At the station, Pat handed the post to Nisha.

"Hiya, Meera," said Julian. "Is your dad around?"

"He's on the other platform. Come on, I'll take you."

Julian told Ajay about his class talk.

"Hop up then, lad!" said Ajay, "and I'll tell you all about being a train-driver."

Julian learnt how to shovel coal into the boiler to stoke up the engine. He tooted the whistle, pulled the lever – and drove the train!

Mr Pringle had just arranged the desks and chairs when the clock struck twelve. The children filed in and sat down.

"Well, as you can see," Jeff smiled, "we have a lovely new shiny classroom floor, thanks to Ted! And now it's Julian's turn to give a class talk!"

Julian stood up and cleared his throat. "Ahem! Today I found out that there are lots of different jobs that need doing in Greendale. . . . Some people make the gardens look nice. . . and make sure the bells ring. . . . Some people make sure we go in the right direction. . . and don't get into trouble. Some people help us to travel to faraway places. . . . And some people like my dad make sure everyone gets their letters on time. . .

. . . and that's what I learnt about jobs!"

The whole class applauded.

"Well done, Julian," said Jeff Pringle, "you made a very good job of 'people's jobs'! I think that deserves a special gold star."

"Yes, well done Julian!" said Pat, who'd been listening at the door.

Suddenly everyone heard a ZZZzzzz coming from the classroom cupboard.

"Miaow!" Jess went to investigate.

And there was Ted, fast asleep!

Pat laughed. "Looks like Ted has been working hard at his job, too!"

SIMON AND SCHUSTER

First published in 2004 in Great Britain by Simon & Schuster UK Ltd
Africa House, 64-78 Kingsway
London WC2B 6AH

Postman Pat® © 2004 Woodland Animations, a division of Entertainment Rights PLC
Licensed by Entertainment Rights PLC
Original writer John Cunliffe
From the original television design by Ivor Wood
Royal Mail and Post Office imagery is used by kind permission of Royal Mail Group plc
All rights reserved

Text by Alison Ritchie © 2004 Simon & Schuster UK Ltd

A CIP catalogue record for this book is available from the British Library upon request

ISBN 0 689 87248 8

Printed in China

3 5 7 9 10 8 6 4 2